獻給艾拉——C.R.
獻給阿波琳——A.S.

♥IREAD

皮皮與波西：生日派對

文　　　字	卡蜜拉‧里德
繪　　　圖	阿克賽爾‧薛弗勒
譯　　　者	酪梨壽司
責任編輯	江奕萱
美術編輯	郭雅萍

發 行 人	劉振強
出 版 者	三民書局股份有限公司
地　　　址	臺北市復興北路 386 號 (復北門市)
	臺北市重慶南路一段 61 號 (重南門市)
電　　　話	(02)25006600
網　　　址	三民網路書店 https://www.sanmin.com.tw

出版日期	初版一刷 2021 年 10 月
書籍編號	S859621
I S B N	978-957-14-7274-4

Text Copyright © Camilla Reid 2021
Illustrations Copyright © Axel Scheffler 2021
Traditional Chinese Copyright © 2021 by San Min Book Co., Ltd.
This translation of Pip and Posy: The Birthday Party is published by
arrangement with Nosy Crow ® Limited

皮皮與波西
生日派對

卡蜜拉·里德／文　阿克賽爾·薛弗勒／圖　酪梨壽司／譯

三民書局

今天是波西的生日。
她非常興奮。

這時，門鈴響了。

「生ㄕㄥ日ㄖ快ㄎㄨㄞ樂ㄌㄜ，波ㄅㄛ西ㄒㄧ！」皮ㄆㄧ皮ㄆㄧ說ㄕㄨㄛ。

他為波西帶來一份
美好的禮物。

「是ㄕ玩ㄨㄢˊ具ㄐㄩˋ公ㄍㄨㄥ車ㄔㄜ！」波ㄅㄛ西ㄒㄧ說ㄕㄨㄛ。

「真ㄓㄣ是ㄕ謝ㄒㄧㄝˋ謝ㄒㄧㄝ你ㄋㄧˇ，皮ㄆㄧˊ皮ㄆㄧ！」

公車真好玩。

但很快就到了派對遊戲時間。

他們先玩了「音樂木頭人」遊戲……

再玩「氣球不落地」遊戲……

捉迷藏 ……

最後是「釘上恐龍尾巴」！

接下來是
午茶時間。

皮皮準備了一個特別的驚喜給波西。

是ㄕ個ㄍㄜ漂ㄆㄧㄠ亮ㄌㄧㄤ的ㄉㄜ生ㄕㄥ日ㄖ蛋ㄉㄢ糕ㄍㄠ！

但當皮皮走向餐桌時，
他踩到了玩具公車。

皮皮跌了一大跤，

蛋糕也跟著
飛出去！

可憐的皮皮。

可憐的波西。

可憐的蛋糕。

天啊，天啊，喔，天啊！

「我很抱歉，波西，」
皮皮說。
「妳的蛋糕毀了。」

「但這不是你的錯，皮皮，」波西抽泣著說
「這是個意外。」

他們決定把東西收拾乾淨。

很快的，一切看起來好多了。

皮皮想到了一個好點子。

「我們來做新蛋糕吧。」他說。

於是他們一起做蛋糕。

他們為大家都做了新蛋糕。

波西得到三個蛋糕！

生日快樂，波西！

太棒啦！

It was Posy's birthday.
She was very excited.

Just then, the doorbell rang.

He had brought Posy
a lovely present.

"Happy Birthday, Posy!" said Pip.

"A bus!" said Posy.

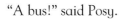

"Thank you so much, Pip!"

The bus was lots of fun.

But soon it was time for the party games.

First, they played musical statues…

then keep-the-balloons-in-the-air…

hide-and-seek…

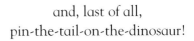

and, last of all,
pin-the-tail-on-the-dinosaur!

Then it was teatime.

Soon, Pip had a very special surprise for Posy.

It was a beautiful birthday cake!

But as Pip was walking to the table, he stepped on the bus.

Pip flew into the air…

and so did the cake!

Poor Pip.

Poor Posy.

Poor cake.

Oh dear, oh dear, oh DEAR!

"I'm sorry, Posy," said Pip.
"Your cake is ruined."

"But it wasn't your fault, Pip," sniffed Posy.
"It was an accident."

They decided to tidy up.

And soon everything looked much better.

Then Pip had a good idea.

"Let's make new cakes," he said.

And that's what they did.

They made new cakes for everybody.

And THREE for Posy!

Happy birthday, Posy!

Hooray!

卡蜜拉·里德　Camilla Reid

卡蜜拉·里德在出版界資歷超過20年，長期致力於為小讀者們創造優質圖書。自從生了兩位小寶貝以後，她也逐漸在奇特且迷人的幼兒領域培養起敏銳洞察力，陸續創作了許多暢銷的繪本、操作書和圖文書。

阿克賽爾·薛弗勒　Axel Scheffler

1957年出生於德國漢堡市，25歲時前往英國就讀巴斯藝術學院。他的插畫風格幽默又不失優雅，最著名的當屬《古飛樂》(Gruffalo) 系列作品，不僅榮獲英國多項繪本大獎，譯作超過40種語言，還曾改編為動畫，深受全球觀眾喜愛，是世界知名的繪本作家。薛弗勒現居英國，持續創作中。

酪梨壽司

當過記者、玩過行銷，在紐約和東京流浪多年後，終於返鄉定居的臺灣媽媽。出沒於臉書專頁「酪梨壽司」與個人部落格「酪梨壽司的日記」。